Home Sweet Home

Creepy Crawlies

Join the Creepy Crawlies in all their
fun-packed adventures!

 Be sure to read:

The Talent Contest

... and lots, lots more!

Home Sweet Home

Tony Bradman
illustrated by Damon Burnard

SCHOLASTIC

For Stephanie

Scholastic Children's Books,
Commonwealth House, 1-19 New Oxford Street,
London, WC1A 1NU, UK
a division of Scholastic Ltd
London ~ New York ~ Toronto ~ Sydney ~ Auckland
Mexico City ~ New Delhi ~ Hong Kong

First published by Scholastic Ltd, 2004

ISBN 0 439 97775 4

Printed and bound by Tien Wah Press Pte. Ltd, Singapore

10 9 8 7 6 5 4 3 2

Chapter One

In a corner of The Garden, beyond The
Flower Bed and underneath The Big Bush,
there stood a little house … where one little
creature wasn't too happy.

Lucy the Ladybird lived with her three friends – Billy the Beetle, Doug the Slug and Imelda the Centipede.  But she was the only one who ever did anything around the house, and she was getting fed up with it.

Today, for instance, she had tidied the living room, which the others had made very messy the day before…

Then she'd done *their* washing and pegged *their* wet clothes on the line…

And now she was mopping the kitchen floor.

"Work, work, work," she muttered to herself. "That's all I ever do. But does anyone care? I don't think so. There, finished at last, thank goodness."

The floor was clean and shiny and sparkling, just the way Lucy liked it.

Suddenly the back door opened with a bang, and Billy ran in.

"Hi, Lucy," he said, dashing past her. "Been jogging round The Smelly Pond. I feel *great!*" Then he crashed through the other door and was gone.

Lucy looked at the trail of footprints Billy had made across the kitchen floor with his muddy trainers. She scowled, and marched out after him. But she wasn't prepared for the scene she found in the living room.

GGRR!

Doug was slumped on the sofa watching TV. He was eating popcorn, and had dropped lots of bits on the floor. He had also scattered his comics and computer games everywhere, and had even knocked over a pot plant.

Not that he'd noticed. He did notice Lucy at the door, though.

"Hey, Lucy," he said. "When will lunch be ready? I'm starving."

"Me too," said Billy. He slumped down next to Doug and planted his muddy trainers on the coffee table.

"I don't believe it…" Lucy said. "I only tidied up in here an hour ago!"

Then Imelda came strolling in. "Oh good, there you are, Lucy!" she said. "I'm going out soon, and I haven't got a thing to wear. Just iron my yellow dress for me, will you?"

Lucy stared at them. She threw down the mop and yelled,

THAT'S IT! I'VE HAD ENOUGH!

Then she turned round and stomped off upstairs.

The other three looked at each other, their mouths open in surprise.

Chapter Two

"Please, Lucy," said Billy. "We know something's wrong, but we can't do much about it if you won't talk to us. You've been in there for ages."

Billy, Doug and Imelda were standing on the landing outside Lucy's room. Her door was shut, and beyond it there was silence.

"Besides," Doug moaned. "Isn't it time you cooked our lunch?"

"And what about my dress?" said Imelda. "I don't want to be late…"

The door flew open and Lucy strode out. She looked as if she were about to explode. Billy, Doug and Imelda quickly took several steps backwards.

"And *I* don't want to do all the work around here any more," Lucy snapped. "I'm fed up with it. *I* can't do the things *I'd* like to do…

Because I'm forever doing the cooking, and washing, and ironing, and tidying up after you lot…and you don't care a bit!

She stomped back into her room, and slammed the door shut behind her with a …

BANG!

Billy, Doug and Imelda returned to the living room.

"Oooooh," said Imelda. "Who hit her with the grumpy stick, then?"

"I have an awful feeling we might not get any lunch," Doug moaned.

"Hang on a minute, you two," said Billy. "Lucy's got a point, you know. We don't do much to help around the house. And that's not very fair, is it?"

Imelda shrugged.

Billy shrugged too.

Doug looked
worried.

"It's simple," said Billy. "I think we should
do more. A lot more."

"You can't possibly be serious," said
Imelda, her eyes wide as, well ... as wide as
a bug's.

You think we should
actually do some
of the housework?

"What, like tidying up and cleaning?"
Doug said, looking disgusted.
"Er … no thanks.
I barely have
time to watch all
my favourite
TV shows
as it is."

"And I barely have time for my beauty routine every day," said Imelda. "You don't seem to realize that some things are very important, Billy."

"Oh, but I do," said Billy. "In fact, I've realized that one of the most important things is making sure we don't take our friend for granted. So, the sooner we get started, the better. Right, guys?"

Imelda and Doug didn't reply. They didn't look convinced, either.

"Come on, you two," said Billy. "After all, it's the only way we can show Lucy that we *do* care about her. Oh, and er … not to mention the only way you'll get your dress ironed, Imelda, or that you'll get any lunch, Doug."

Suddenly, Imelda and Doug seemed much more interested in the idea.

Chapter Three

A little while later, Lucy emerged from her room and stomped downstairs. It was quiet in the living room, and no one seemed to be there.

Then Billy popped up from behind the sofa. He smiled nervously at Lucy.

"Lucy! Er … hi!" he spluttered. "I, er …
just wanted to say…"

"Don't think you can get round me by
begging," Lucy said in her snootiest voice.
She sniffed and turned her back on him.
"I simply won't listen."

"Actually, I wasn't going to beg," said
Billy. "I was about to say you're right, and
we're sorry, and we'll be doing a lot more
to help from now on."

"What, you three?" said Lucy. "I'll believe *that* when I see it."

"We will, honest," said Billy. "Look, I'm tidying in here. I've picked up the pot plant and the popcorn and the comics and the games… Oh, whoops!"

Billy had tripped over the table and made a mess again, and he could tell Lucy wasn't impressed.

She wasn't impressed by what she saw in the kitchen, either. Imelda was ironing her dress, and Doug was cooking the lunch.

Although neither of them seemed to be getting on that well...

"Nice work..." said Lucy. "I *don't* think. I'm off to have some fun."

And with that, she swept out of the little house, her nose in the air.

"Oh dear," said Billy. "It looks like we'll just have to try harder."

So that's what they did. Billy organized them, and they all helped each other…

…and over the next few days they began to get the hang of things.

Soon Billy and Doug even started to enjoy themselves.

Imelda did too – until Billy said she should tidy her room and put away her clothes … *and* her shoes.

"You have *got* to be joking!" said Imelda. Billy just gave her a look. "Oh, all right," Imelda sighed. "Now I know what being a fashion victim means…"

Lucy came and went, and wouldn't speak to them. Although by the end of the week, Billy was certain he'd caught her looking surprised once or twice.

And there had been a strange expression on her face a couple of times, too…

At last the house was *so* clean and tidy –
except for Imelda's room, of course – that
Doug felt he had to say something.

He'd just finished hoovering the living
room when Lucy walked in.

Hi Lucy!

"Not bad, eh?" said Doug, proudly.
"There, Lucy, you didn't think we'd
change, but we have!"

Lucy's bottom lip quivered.

Then she burst into tears and ran upstairs.

Chapter Four

"For heaven's sake," said Doug when the others came in to find out what was going on. "What's wrong with her now? She should be pleased, shouldn't she? You know, I don't understand ladybirds, and I never will."

"Well, she obviously isn't," said Billy. "And we need to find out why."

"Shush!" said Doug. "I think I can hear her coming back downstairs."

Doug was right. In fact, Lucy *ran* down the stairs. Billy noticed she was still upset, but she dashed out of the house before he could say anything.

"We'd better go after her and make sure she's all right," said Billy.

"Do we have to?" Doug moaned. "*The Garden Rock Show* is on soon."

"We most certainly do," said Billy crossly. "Right – Doug, you come with me, and Imelda, you stay here and finish tidying your room. How are you getting on up there?"

"Er … not great, Billy," sighed Imelda.

"You've got till we come back," said Billy. "OK Doug, let's go!"

Billy led the way. Luckily, Lucy hadn't got very far ahead. She was hurrying along the path towards The Garden Mall, her shoulders hunched. She was muttering, too. Billy slipped into the bushes at the side of the path and crept along, listening to her. Doug stayed close behind him.

"So now they think they can do everything," Lucy was saying. "Huh, well, what do I care? Let them! That means I can spend all my time having fun!"

"Hmm…" thought Billy. "But it sounds to me like she *does* care."

Billy wanted to hear what else their friend might mutter to herself. So they kept following her, right up to the entrance to The Garden Mall, and inside.

They followed her to the library…

…to Mrs Buzzy Bee's Coffee Shop…

…and to Bella Butterfly's Beauty Parlour,
where Lucy had her wings buffed.

And Billy made absolutely certain she
didn't see them,
not once.

"This is *so* cool," Doug whispered. "We're like spies on a mission!"

"Be quiet, Doug!" Billy hissed crossly at him. "I can't hear her."

"But what if it means they don't need me any more?" Lucy was saying quietly to herself.

"Ah," murmured Billy. "I think I understand the problem now…"

Chapter Five

"It's no good, Billy, you'll have to explain it again," Doug said later as Billy hurried him back to the little house. "For a moment there I thought I understood what you were saying…" Doug said, frowning. "Er … then I got confused."

When they got home Imelda came rushing downstairs. She looked worn out, although very pleased with herself.

"Phew, I've done it," she murmured, almost as if she couldn't believe what she was saying. "I've actually tidied my room. You should see it, Billy…"

"Well, you can just go back upstairs and untidy it," said Billy.

"Now I'm really confused," Doug said. "Or maybe I'm dreaming."

WHAT!

"I'm sorry?" said Imelda. "You want me to *untidy* my room? Why?"

"We'll have to untidy the living room," Billy was murmuring, not taking any notice of her, "and then perhaps we could spill stuff in the kitchen…"

"Billy, talk to me!" Imelda yelled.

"Look, it's simple," said Billy. "We've gone way too far. We've got so good at doing the housework that Lucy is worried we don't need her any more... So we have to show her that we *do*." Billy paused.

Doug looked totally stunned, and
Imelda's face was stony.

"I know it sounds crazy," said Billy at last.
"But you'll just have to trust me on this one.
OK, guys?"

Doug and Imelda glanced at each other,
then back at Billy.

"OK," they sighed together. "What do
you want us to do?"

When Lucy came home, a horrifying
sight met her eyes.
The kitchen
was a mess…

The living room
was a totally,
terrible mess…

In fact, the whole house was a mess,
including Imelda's room,
which looked exactly
the same as it
usually did.

"Oh, hi, Lucy," said Doug. He was slumped on the sofa, watching TV.

"Er … sorry about all this," said Billy. "We just don't seem able to keep on top of things the way *you* used to."

Billy nudged Doug.

"What?" said Doug.

"Oh yeah, we're useless."

"Hah! I knew you wouldn't be able to manage without me!" said Lucy. "So … I suppose you want me to take over and do everything, right?"

They could all see she was trying hard not to smile or sound eager.

"We'd love you to be in charge," Billy said. "But we'll help too!"

"Well … all right," said Lucy, grinning now. "Let's get cracking! Doug, you start in the living room, and Imelda, you can go and tidy your room, and Billy, well, you can…"

Doug looked wistfully at the TV, and
Imelda sighed. "Home sweet
home," she muttered,
trudging upstairs.

And that's just what it was. For the time
being, anyway…